Jessica Souhami made her first shadow puppets in 1968 while
a student at the Central School of Art and Design.
In 1980 she formed Mme Souhami & Co, a travelling puppet company
using brightly coloured shadow puppets with a musical accompaniment
and a storyteller. *The Leopard's Drum* is an adaptation of
one of the company's most successful productions.
Old MacDonald, her second book for Frances Lincoln, was published in 1996.

First Published in Great Britain in 1995 by
Frances Lincoln Limited, 4 Torriano Mews,
Torriano Avenue, London NW5 2RZ

British Library Cataloguing in Publication Data available on request

ISBN 0-7112-0906-5 hardback
ISBN 0-7112-0907-3 paperback

Set in Monotype News Plantin

Printed in Hong Kong

1 3 5 7 9 8 6 4 2

THE LEOPARD'S DRUM

With thanks to Amoafi Kwapong and Peter Sarpong

Jessica Souhami

THE LEOPARD'S DRUM

An Asante tale from West Africa

FRANCES LINCOLN

Osebo, the leopard, was fierce, proud, and boastful.

He made a huge drum and he played it every day.

Animals came from near and far to see it.

It was a magnificent drum, the best they had ever seen.

They all wished it belonged to them.

Even Nyame, the Sky-God, wanted it.

   "Osebo," he said, "that's a wonderful drum.

I should have a drum like that. Will you give me your drum?"

   "No," said Osebo.

   "Will you lend me your drum?"

   "No!" said Osebo.

"Will you let me try your drum?"

But Osebo said, "NO!"

"You should respect me, Osebo. I am the Sky-God.
Animals of the forest, whoever brings me that drum will get
a big reward."

And Nyame disappeared.

Next day Onini, the python, went to get the drum.

"Looking for me, Onini?"
"Oh, er – no, Osebo...
just looking at your fine drum,
your huge drum,
your magnificent drum...
Good-day, Osebo."

Next day Esono, the elephant, went to get the drum.

"Looking for me, Esono?"

"Oh, er – no, Osebo.
Just admiring your fine drum,
your huge drum,
your **magnificent** drum, Osebo.
Goodbye, Osebo."

The next day,
something strange
moved slowly through
the forest.

The animals were puzzled.
Some were frightened.
"What is it?" they whispered.
"Whoever can it be?"

It was Asroboa, the monkey,
going to get the drum.
He hoped Osebo wouldn't see him
behind the mask.

"Looking for me, Asroboa?"
"Ohhh no, Osebo.
Just looking...fine...huge...
mag...ni...fi...cen...t..."

Last of all Achi-cheri, the tortoise,
went to get Osebo's drum.
    "You haven't got a chance,"
the other animals said, "not a titchy little,
weedy little creature like you!"

It was true, the tortoise was very small,
and in those days her shell was quite soft.
She had to watch out that careless animals
didn't squash her flat.

"Well, I'm going to try anyway," she said.

"Looking for me, Achi-cheri?"

"Not really, Osebo. I was just looking at this drum."

"Don't you think it's a fine, huge, magnificent drum, Achi-cheri?"

"Well, it's all right, I suppose, for a middle-sized kind of drum, Osebo."

"**Middle-sized?** You ridiculous creature, don't you know this is the biggest, the best drum in the forest?"

"Well," said Achi-cheri, "I've heard that Nyame's got a bigger drum."

"What!" said Osebo.

"Oh yes. It's so big, he can climb right inside it and not one bit of him sticks out."

"Well, I can climb right inside mine," said Osebo. "Just watch."

Osebo began to squeeze himself into the drum.

"Am I inside, Achi-cheri?"

"No, not nearly, Osebo."

"Now, Achi-cheri?"

"No, not quite, Osebo."

"Now, Achi-cheri?"

"Yes, Osebo, now you're inside. But you can't get out!"
And Achi-cheri sealed the drum with a large cooking pot.

"Now I'm going to take you to the Sky-God."

Slowly, Achi-cheri pushed the enormous drum with the heavy
leopard inside it all the way to Nyame.

"Here is Osebo's drum, Nyame. And Osebo is inside."

"Well done!" said Nyame. "No-one else could get the drum. And you have taught that boastful leopard a lesson. Let him go now, and decide what you would like as your reward."

Achi-cheri looked round. All the other animals were looking jealous and cross. She thought for a moment.

"Please, Nyame," she said, "most of all I would like a hard shell to protect me from fierce animals."

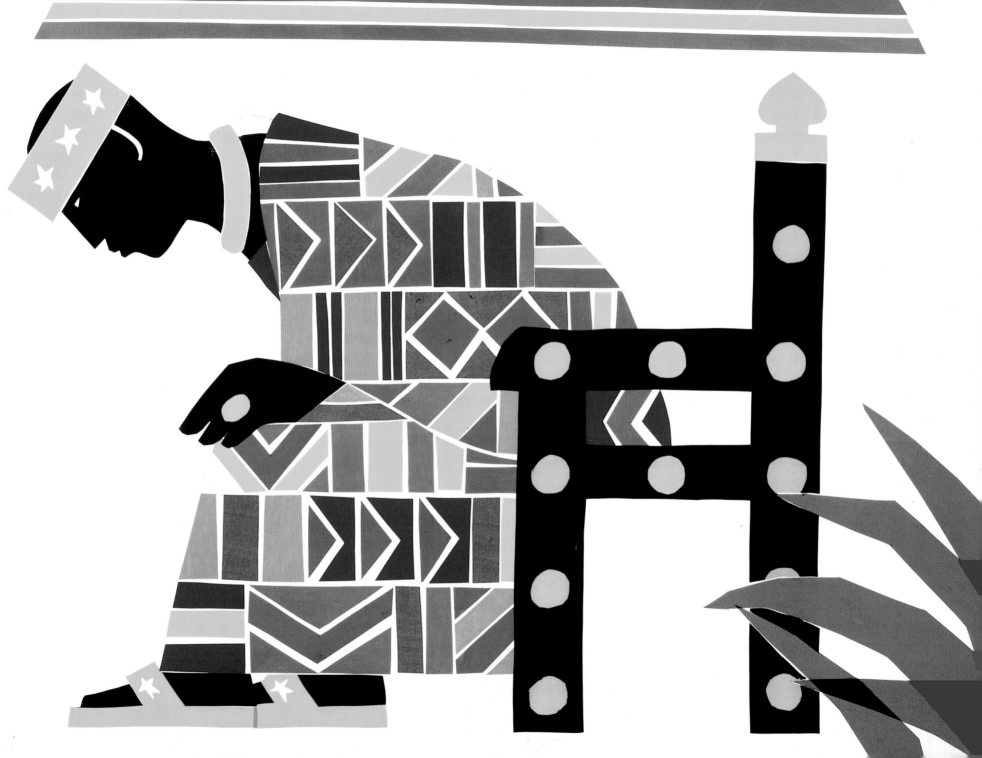

Nyame laughed and gave her a tough, hard shell.
And Achi-cheri the tortoise still wears it today.

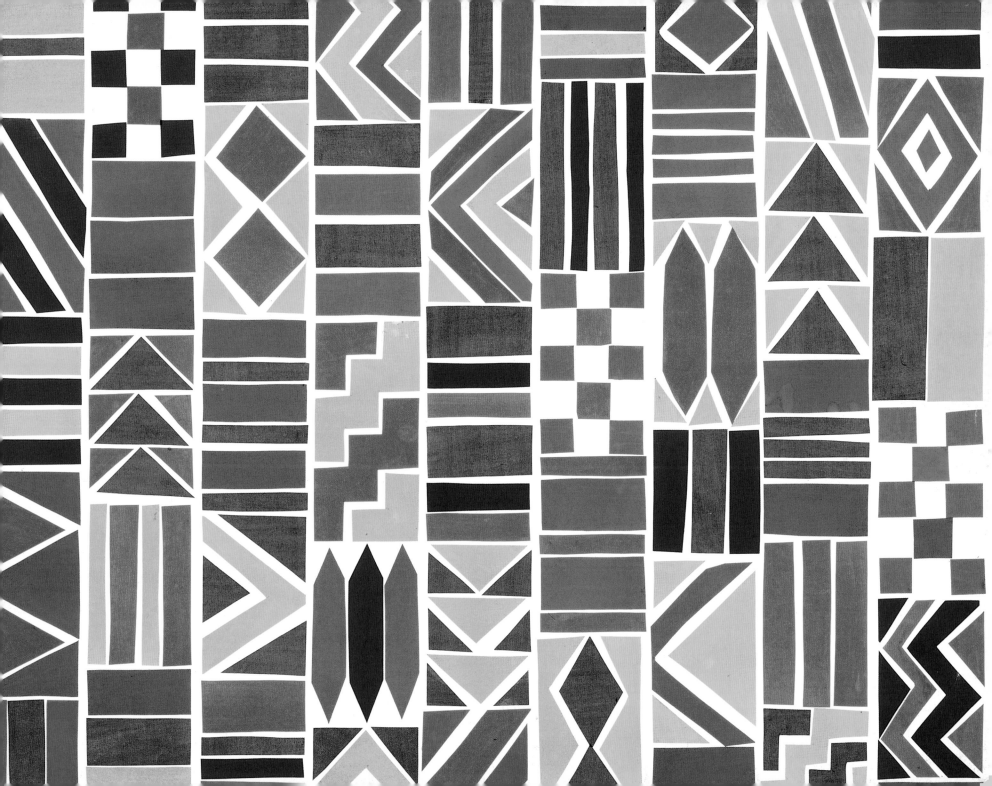

MORE PICTURE BOOKS IN PAPERBACK FROM FRANCES LINCOLN

OLD MACDONALD
Jessica Souhami

Old MacDonald's Farm is full of surprises. What's that in the pram? Who's flying a plane?
What's got four arms and goes 'beep'? Lift the five surprise flaps and see for yourself - then open out
the final page for a deafening finale! A fun first book for the very young.

Suitable for National Curriculum English - Reading, Key Stage 1
Scottish Guidelines English Language - Reading, Talking and Listening, Level A
ISBN 0-7112-1086-1 £4.99

THE BIG STORM
Dave and Julie Saunders

Dark clouds are gathering over the wood. "Hide and shelter!" cry the animals one by one,
running into their holes and burrows. As the storm breaks, the Squirrels find an unlikely
hiding-place and, when the rain stops, a surprise treasure-trove as well!

Suitable for National Curriculum English - Reading, Key Stage 1
Scottish Guidelines English Language - Reading, Level A
ISBN 0-7112-0865-4 £3.99

NUMBER PARADE
Jakki Wood

One slow tortoise, five rollicking, rascally racoons, ten bouncing, bopping wallabies...Jakki Wood's
birds and beasts gain multiples and momentum as the score mounts to 101 in this wildlife counting book.

Suitable for National Curriculum Mathematics, Key Stage 1
Scottish Guidelines Mathematics, Level A
ISBN 0-7112-0905-7 £3.99

Frances Lincoln titles are available from all good bookshops.
Prices are correct at time of publication, but may be subject to change.